To: The Master Painter and His apprentices — Mom and Dad
From: Your sketch
With love and gratitude.
and
To my dear friend Candid,
and children everywhere.
—Brynne

❀

To my son, Alexander.
—Annika

Illustrator's Acknowledgment
Thanks to my "contributing artists" Alexander, Camryn, Cody, Pablo, and Mylee.

Text Copyright © 2011 Brynne Barnes
Illustration Copyright © 2011 Annika M. Nelson

Sleeping Bear Press™
2395 South Huron Parkway, Suite 200
Ann Arbor, MI 48104
www.sleepingbearpress.com

Printed and bound in the United States.

10 9 8 7 6 5 4 3 2 1

Library of Congress Cataloging-in-Publication Data

Barnes, Brynne, 1983-
Colors of me / written by Brynne Barnes ; illustrated by Annika M. Nelson.
p. cm.
ISBN 978-1-58536-541-8
1. Human skin color—Juvenile literature. 2. Color—Juvenile literature.
I. Nelson, Annika M., 1968- II. Title.
GN197.B37 2011
599.9'45—dc22   2010052911

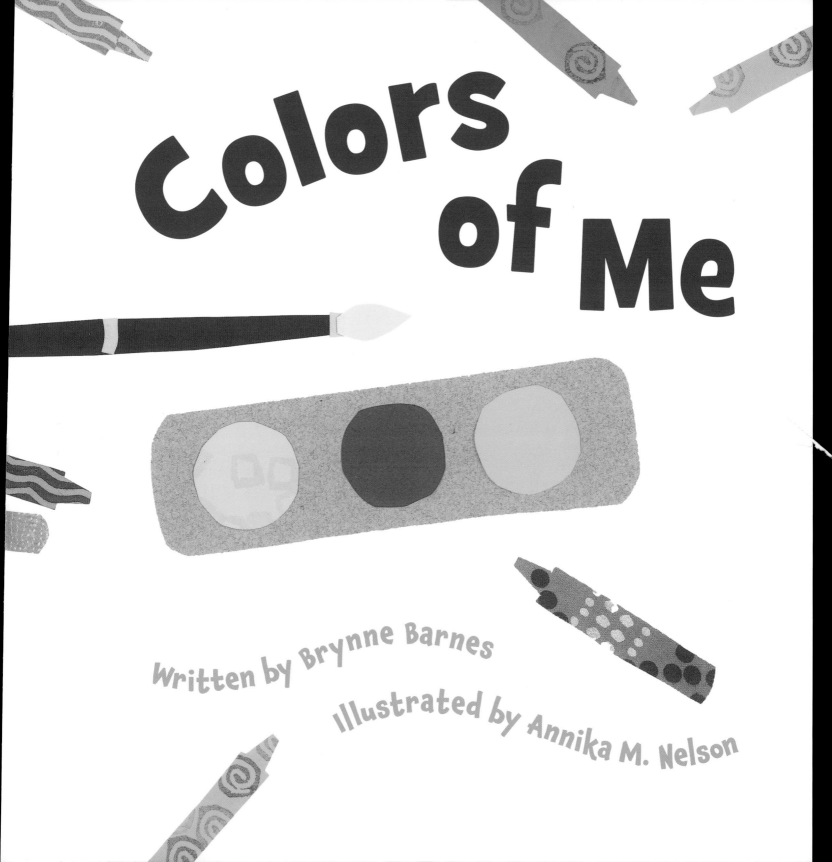

Colors of Me

Written by Brynne Barnes

Illustrated by Annika M. Nelson

I'm coloring the world
    in these pictures that I drew.
What colors should I be?
        Which crayons should I choose?

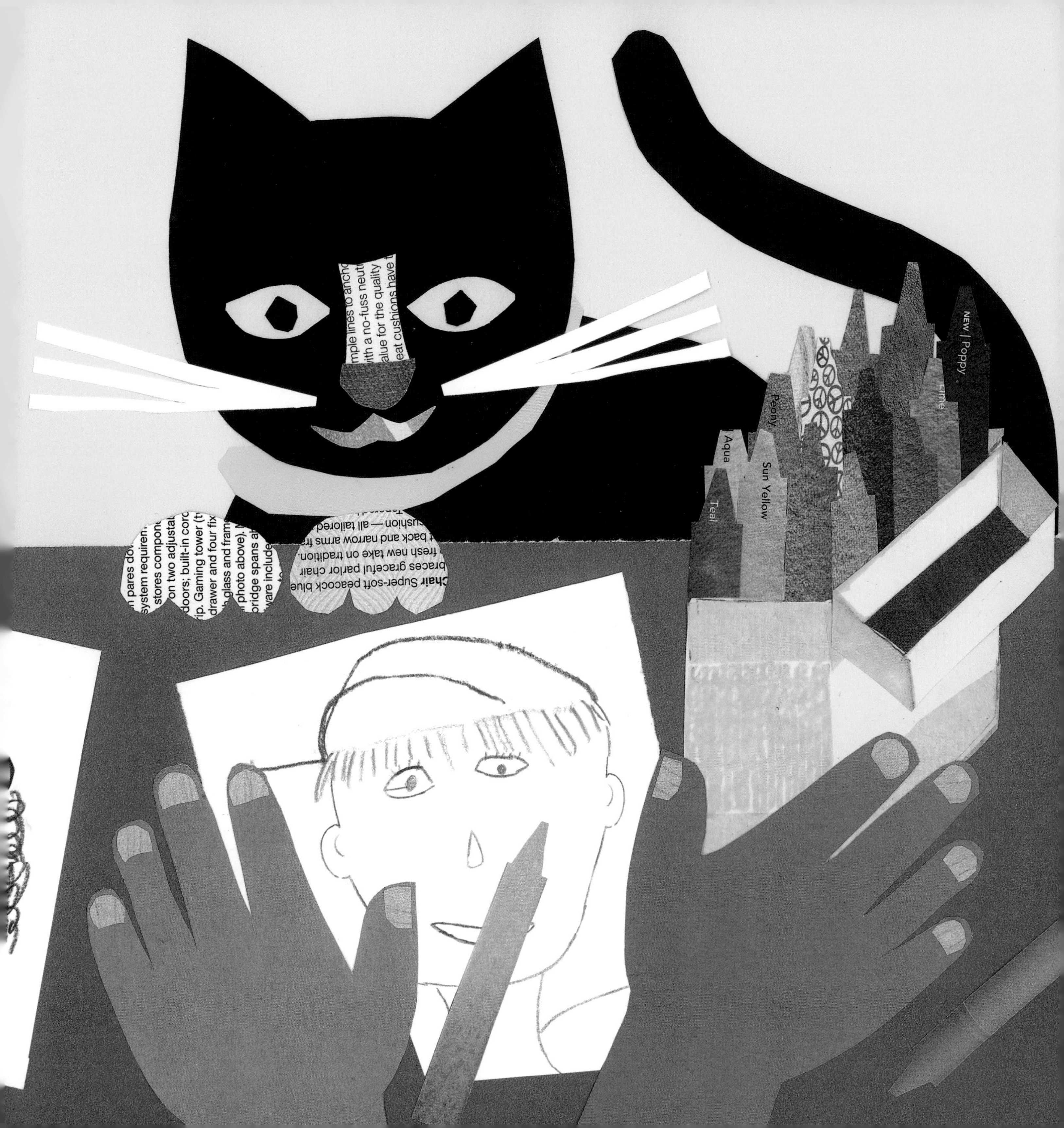
NEW | Poppy
Lime
Peony
Aqua
Sun Yellow
Teal

What color am I to the sky?
What color am I in my dreams?

What color am I to the moon?
What color am I to the sea?

Does the rain think I'm a color
when it falls on my head?

Do the clouds think I'm a color?
Maybe they think I'm green or blue or red.

Does the grass know it's green?
Does the sky know it's blue?

Does the rain have a color?
If it did, would it still make puddles, too?

If flowers had no color,

would they smell as sweet?

Does the sun know the sky turned purple before it went to sleep?

If the trunks of trees were blue and orange
would they grow so tall?

I think I'd climb them either way—
   if they were any color at all.

Do butterflies know the colors of their wings
or only that they can fly?
The world is full of growing, walking, flying colors
that paint the earth and sky.

I can't help but wonder... which ones am I?

When kittens play,

do they wonder about the color of their string?

Can crayons make colors
that laugh, play, and sing?

Do I have to choose one color? I want to be them all!
Orange, brown, blue, purple, pink,
yellow, red, black, white, and green.
The whole world is full of colors—

Brynne Barnes

Brynne Barnes knows a secret: the whole world is a giant coloring book, and the most beautifully potent crayons are words, laughter, and song. Since earning her bachelor of science from the University of Michigan and master of arts degree from Eastern Michigan University, she has been coloring the world with her pen from Ann Arbor, Michigan, where she writes stories like this one, as well as poetry and music. She also teaches writing at Adrian College. This is her first picture book.

Annika M. Nelson

Specializing in collage, block print, and scratch-board, Annika M. Nelson crosses cultural borders, stimulates dialogue between generations, and portrays images of everyday life and the environment in her work. She has illustrated several books and covers, and has done work for many national and international publications. Annika has received commissions for a number of public art installations ranging from interactive murals to a sculpture series permanently installed in the Tidelands Park in Coronado, California. She lives in Southern California.